Guest Spot

CW00498533

THE RAT PACK

Playalong *for* Alto Saxophone

Wise Publications
part of The Music Sales Group
London/New York/Paris/Sydney/Copenhagen/Berlin/Madrid/Tokyo

Published by
Wise Publications
14-15 Berners Street, London W1T 3LJ, UK.

Exclusive Distributors:
Music Sales Limited
Distribution Centre, Newmarket Road, Bury St. Edmunds,
Suffolk IP33 3YB, UK.
Music Sales Pty Limited
20 Resolution Drive, Caringbah, NSW 2229, Australia.

Order No. AM983378
ISBN 1-84609-173-X

Arranging and Engraving supplied by Camden Music.
Edited by Ann Farmer.
Cover photography by George Taylor.
Printed in Great Britain.

CD recorded, mixed and mastered by Jonas Persson.
Instrumental solos by John Whelan.

Band Arrangements by Christopher Hussey and Jeremy Birchall.

Flute/Alto Saxophone: John Whelan.
Clarinet/Tenor Saxophone: Jamie Talbot.
Trumpets: Tony Fisher & Mike Lovatt.
Trombone: Andy Wood.
Violins: Simon Baggs, Christian Halstead, Anya Birchall & Jeremy Birchall.
Viola: Katherine Shave.
Cello: Louise Dixon.
Piano: Gareth Williams.
Keyboards: Christopher Hussey, Ann Farmer & Jonas Persson.
Guitars/Mandolin: Arthur Dick.
Bass: Paul Morgan.
Drums: Ian Thomas & Ralph Salmins.

Saxophone Fingering Chart

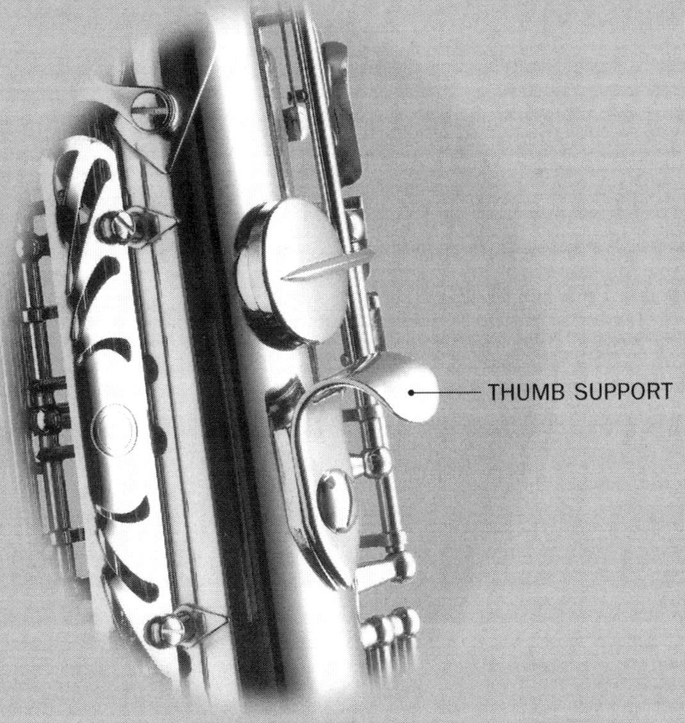

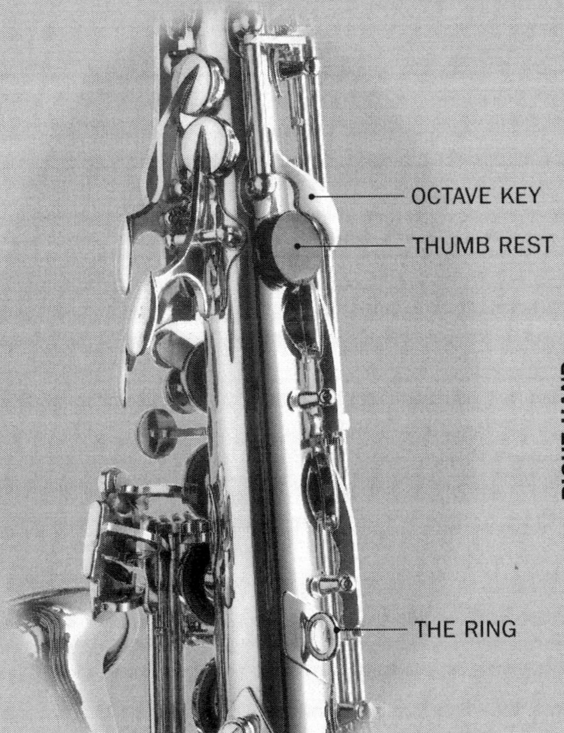

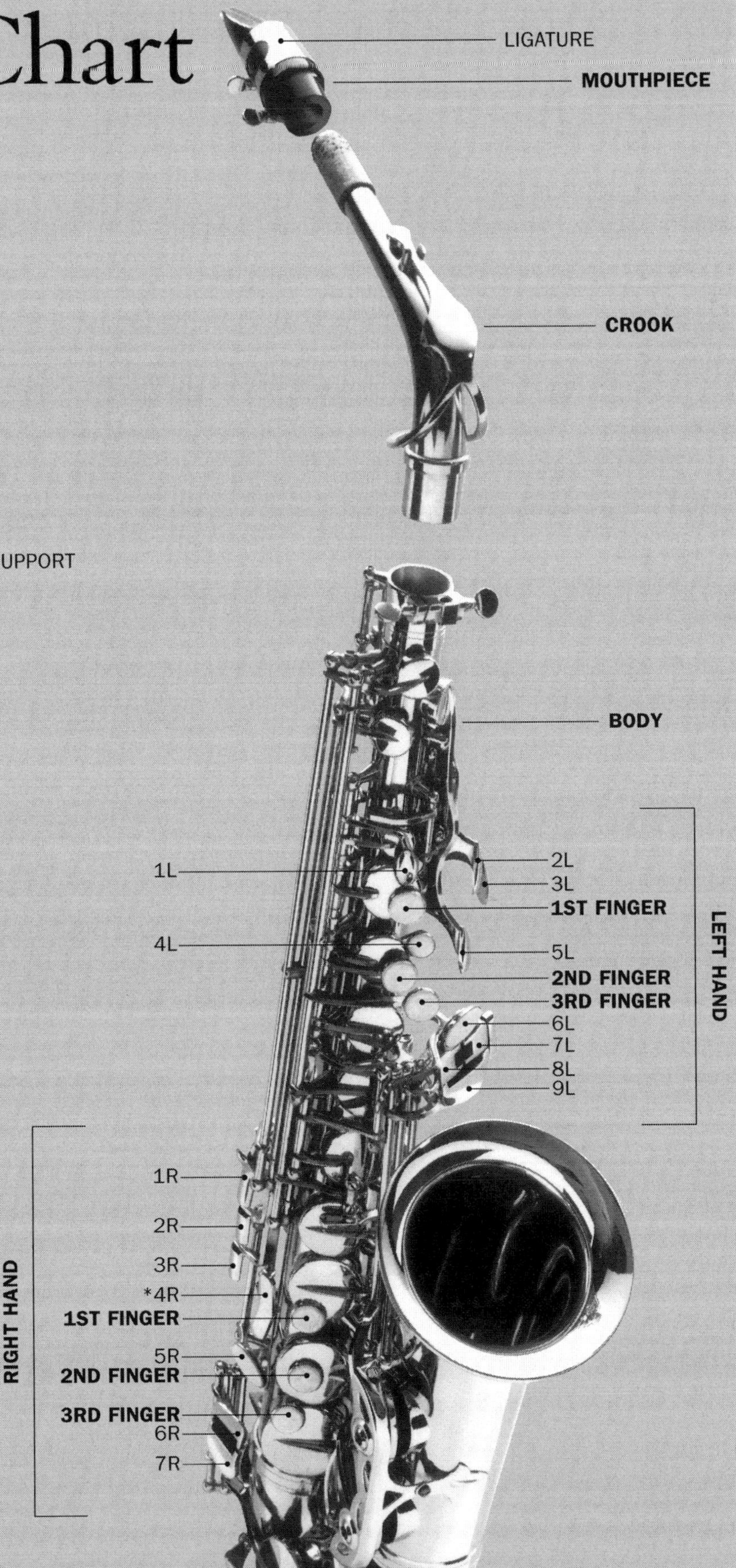

* Not fitted on some saxophones

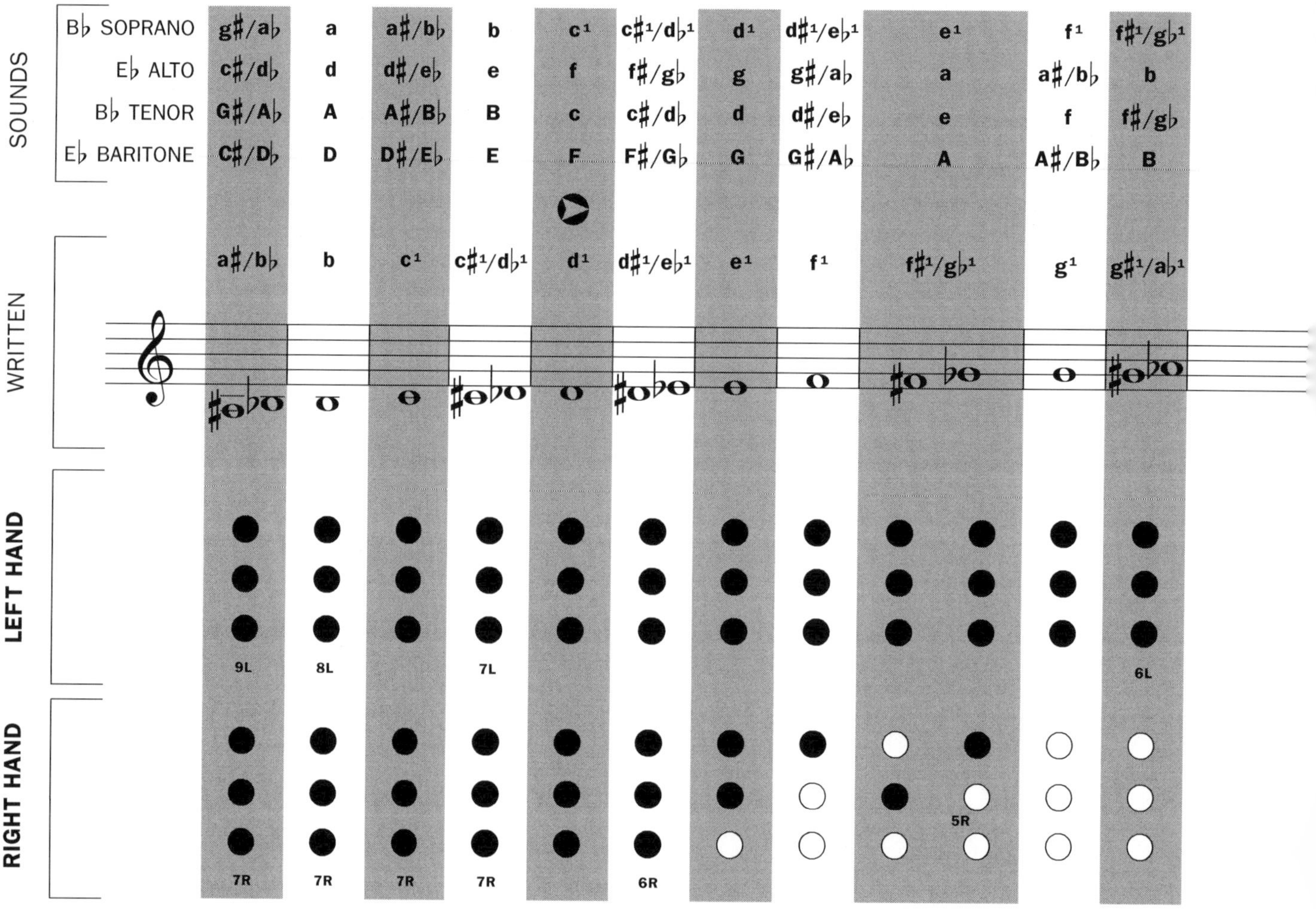

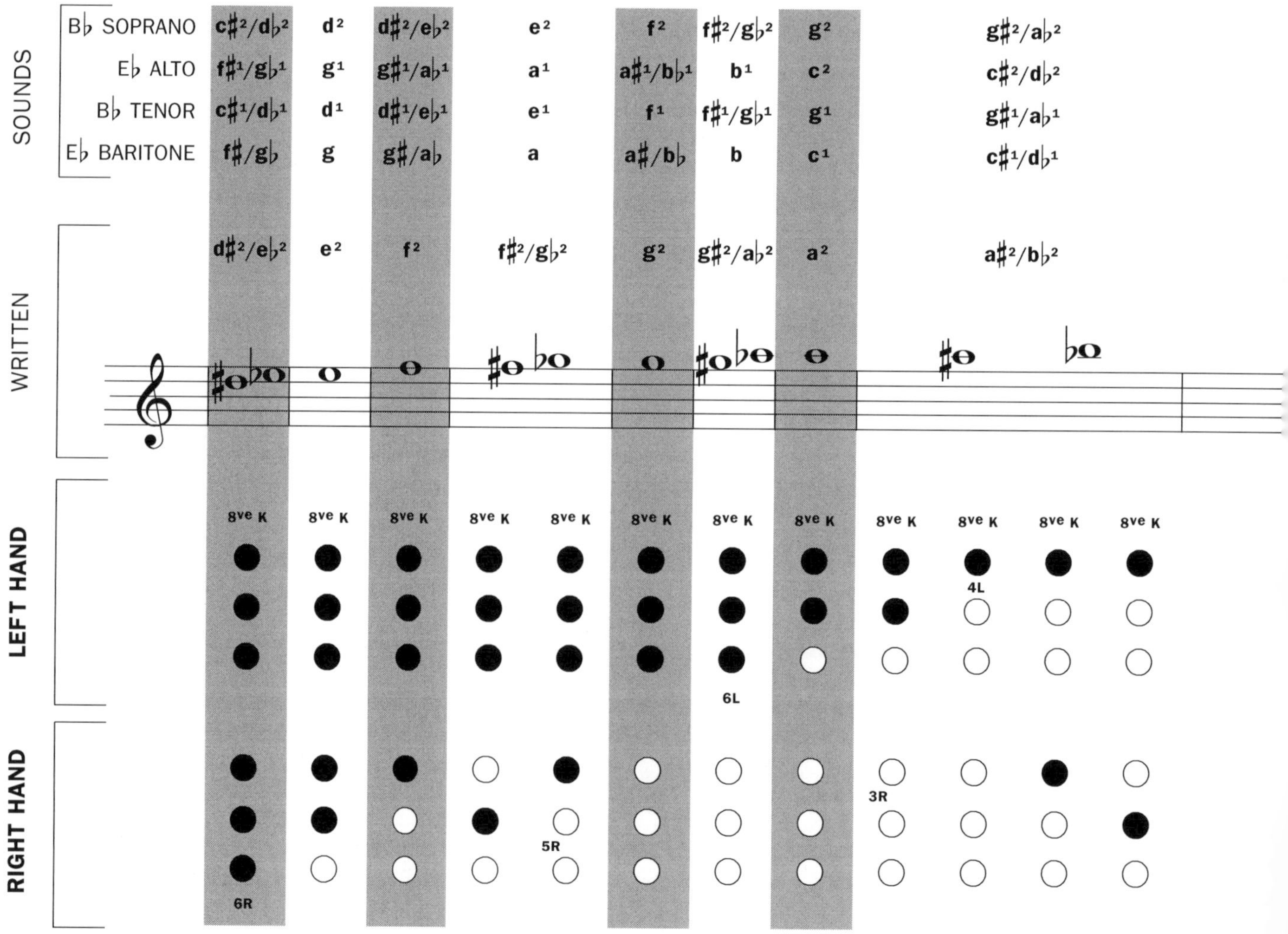

Indicates the lower limit of the best playing range

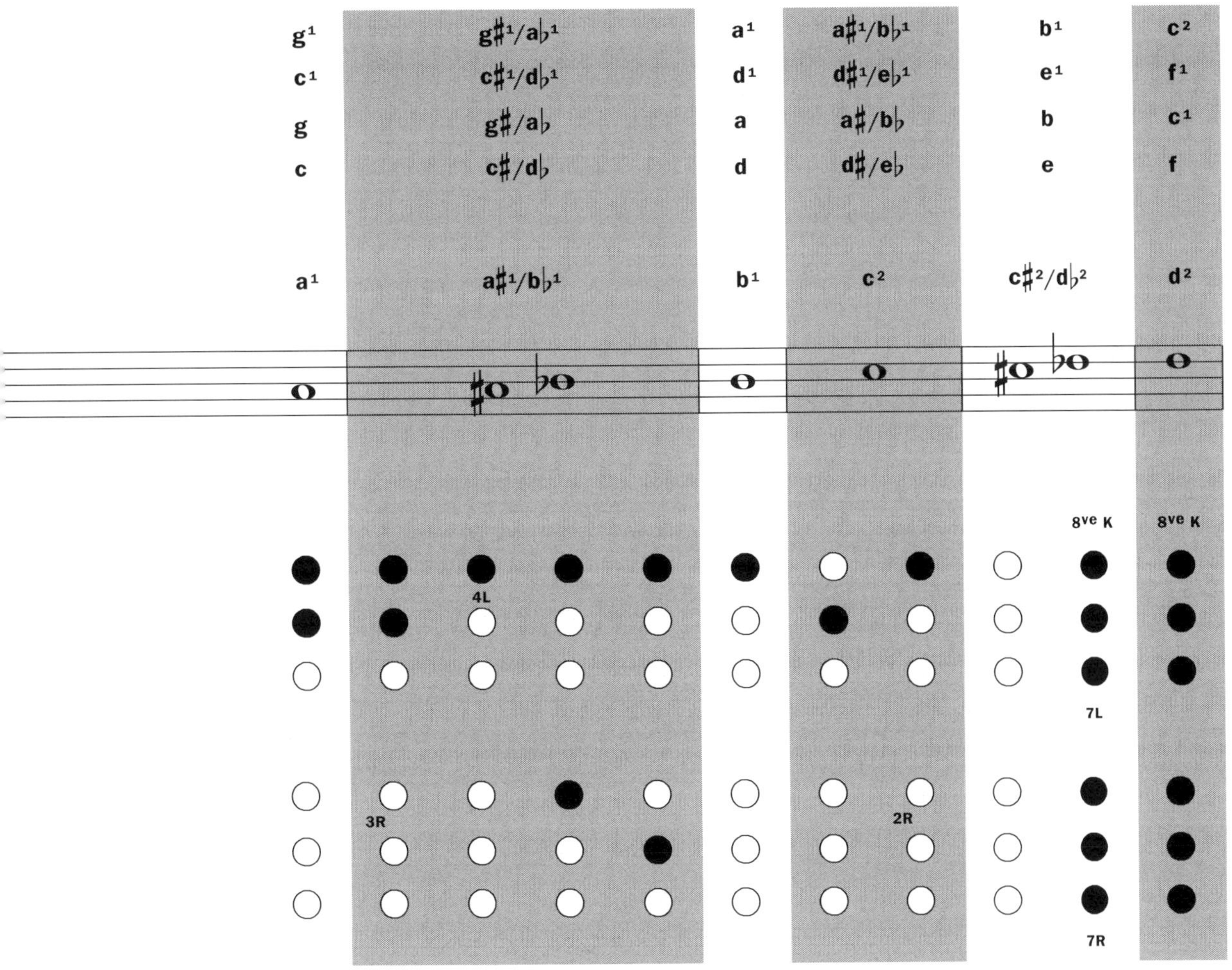

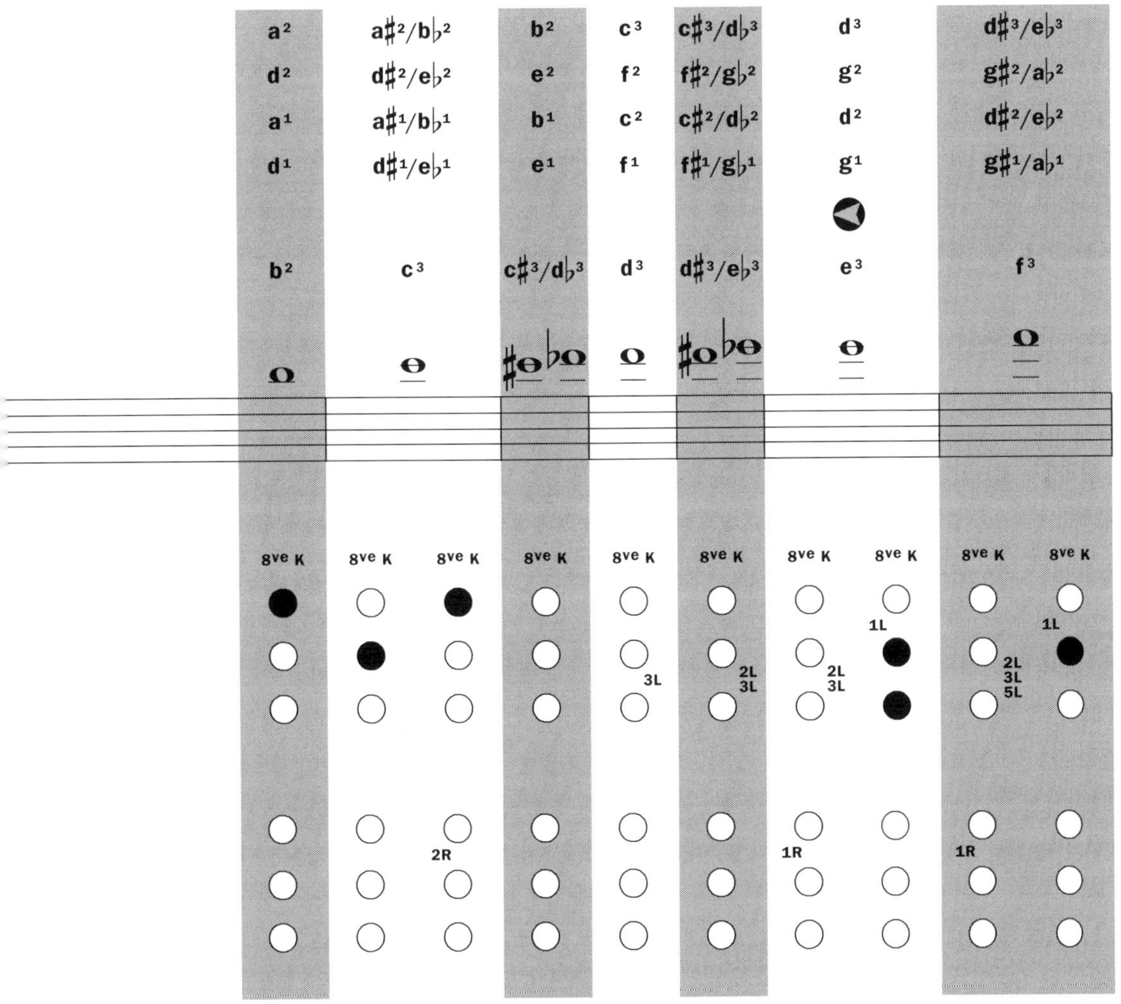

◄ Indicates the upper limit of the best playing range

Ain't That A Kick In The Head

Words by Sammy Cahn
Music by Jimmy Van Heusen

40
mf
44
4
51
f
55
59
ff
mp
64
mf
f
69
74

Come Fly With Me

Words by Sammy Cahn
Music by James Van Heusen

Energetically ♩ = 140

straight ♪s
Instrumental

72
mf
77
82
86
90
95
99
104
tr
sfp

Me And My Shadow

Words by Al Jolson
Music by Billy Rose

19
mf
mp
23
27
mp
mf
31
f
f
mf
mf
36
f
f

41
mf
mp
45
mf
51
55
f
f
59

My Way

Words & Music by Claude Francois, Jacques Revaux & Gilles Thibaut

25
mf
29
33
mf
37
41
45
mp
49

rall.
a tempo ♩ = 69
più mosso ♩ = 92
rall.
a tempo ♩ = 88
slower ♩ = 60

The Lady Is A Tramp

Words by Lorenz Hart
Music by Richard Rodgers

Lazy swing ♩ = 132

33
39
45
50
55
60
65

69
74
80
85
91
95
100

Somethin' Stupid

Words & Music by C. Carson Parks

16
21
25
29
33

37
41
45
Instrumental
7
7
54
Repeat to fade
58

That's Amoré

Words & Music by Harry Warren & Jack Brooks

42
48
56
64
70
rit.
a tempo ♩ = 156
77
82
87

93
99
rit.
a tempo ♩ = 156
105
113
Slower, rubato ♩ = 88
121
a tempo ♩ = 156
128
135
141

(Love Is) The Tender Trap

Words by Sammy Cahn
Music by James Van Heusen

38
42
to Coda
46
49
Instrumental
f
53
2
57
D.S. al Coda
mp
Coda
61
cresc.
65
f
69
mp
f

What Kind Of Fool Am I?

Words & Music by Leslie Bricusse & Anthony Newley

più mosso ♩ = 96
Instrumental
Optional:
8va to end.
cresc.
Freely, slower ♩ = 84
rit.
Slower ♩ = 76
a tempo ♩ = 84

You're Nobody Til Somebody Loves You

Words & Music by Larry Stock, Russ Morgan & James Cavanaugh

Instrumental

CD Track Listing

1. **Tuning Notes**

Full instrumental performances...

2. Ain't That A Kick In The Head
(Cahn/Van Heusen) The International Music Network Limited.

3. Come Fly With Me
(Cahn/Van Heusen) The International Music Network Limited.

4. Me And My Shadow
(Jolson/Dreyer/Rose)
Memory Lane Music Limited/Francis Day & Hunter Limited.

5. My Way
(Revaux/Francois/Thibaut/Anka) SACEM/
Warner/Chappell Music Limited/Warner/Chappell Overseas Holdings.

6. The Lady Is A Tramp
(Rodgers/Hart) Warner/Chappell Music Limited.

7. Somethin' Stupid
(Parks) Montclare Music Company Limited.

8. That's Amoré
(Warren/Brooks) Peermusic (UK) Limited/Famous Music Publishing Limited.

9. (Love Is) The Tender Trap
(Cahn/Van Heusen) The International Music Network Limited.

10. What Kind Of Fool Am I?
(Bricusse/Newley) Tro Essex Music Limited.

11. You're Nobody Till Somebody Loves You
(Stock/Morgan/Cavanaugh) Peermusic (UK) Limited.

Backing tracks only...

12. Ain't That A Kick In The Head
13. Come Fly With Me
14. Me And My Shadow
15. My Way
16. The Lady Is A Tramp
17. Somethin' Stupid
18. That's Amoré
19. (Love Is) The Tender Trap
20. What Kind Of Fool Am I?
21. You're Nobody Till Somebody Loves You

To remove your CD from the plastic sleeve, lift the small lip to break the perforations. Replace the disc after use for convenient storage.